HIGH NOON

Written by Susan Paris
Photographed by Mary Foley

CONTENTS

CHAPTER 1

A SATURDAY GONE WRONG

Eleanor Jessop always woke up on Saturday mornings with a smile on her face. She would wake slowly and lazily, stretching out in her bed. Sometimes she would even say "It's Saturday" out loud to herself, just to enjoy the sound of it.

But, this Saturday morning, Eleanor's mum had woken her noisily, in that bossy way only mums can.

"Get up, Eleanor," her mum hollered into Eleanor's room. "Today's the trip."

Eleanor groaned and snuggled deeper under her bedclothes. She knew what a trip meant. It meant trouble, that's what.

Eleanor's dad was a history teacher at a secondary school on the other side of the city. He loved anything to do with history, and was always trying to teach Eleanor something when she least expected it.

A trip always meant a long ride with Dad, Mum, and Eleanor's little brother, Abraham, to some historic site somewhere out of the city. Her dad always had a really great time, and would bore them silly with historical details the whole way there and the whole way back. It was like a... Well, it was like a history lesson, that's what. And what kid wants a history lesson on a Saturday, thought Eleanor resentfully.

Now her mum's voice snuck in under the covers again, reminding Eleanor for the second time that her Saturday was about to be ruined.

"Come on, Eleanor," called Mum. "Your brother is nearly ready."

Eleanor groaned again. That was the biggest trouble with little brothers. They always had to come, too.

Eleanor's best friend, Sally, always made a huge fuss over Abraham. Eleanor had to admit that he was cute, too cute.

Abraham was eight years old, but very small for his age. He had curly brown hair, freckles, glasses, and big ears that stuck out like an elephant's. Eleanor knew that, if they had been her ears, they would have looked terrible. Somehow, Abraham still managed to look sweet.

That was the problem with being twelve, thought Eleanor. You couldn't rely on being cute any more. Sometimes Eleanor wished she was Abraham. Well, at least she wished she was still eight. When she was that age, Eleanor hadn't minded her father's trips nearly so much.

With a big sigh, Eleanor got up and began getting dressed. She pulled on her favourite jeans, which she always reserved for Saturdays, to cheer herself up. She

remembered all about the trip now. They were going to Goldtown, a reconstructed Wild West town with historic buildings and memorabilia. Eleanor's dad especially loved history about the Wild West. He always watched the old westerns they ran on the movie channel on Sunday afternoons, all the while consuming vast quantities of junk food. Eleanor knew he didn't tell the kids at school about that.

Today her dad was going to be in total history heaven.

Abraham's sneakers thundered down the hallway. He was always eager to go on their dad's trips, and would race all the way to the garage. Once they were on their way to wherever they were going, if Dad wasn't talking, Abraham would be.

Eleanor put her portable CD player in her backpack. Feeling very cross, she went to get some cereal.

Eleanor had to admit to herself that the journey out of the city wasn't so bad. All the open space looked inviting after the crammed, rushed city. Things would almost have been OK, if it weren't for Abraham jiggling about next to her on the back seat. In an attempt to ignore him, Eleanor tried to concentrate on the passing trees. She knew it wasn't going to work.

"Are we there yet?" Abraham yelled.

Abraham liked yelling in small spaces, or so it seemed to Eleanor. In fact, she thought, he specialized in it.

To keep Abraham quiet, Dad stopped for ice cream. Dad was always in a very good mood on their trips, and usually let them have whatever they wanted. For Abraham, it was always ice cream. This time, he came back to the car with an ice cream that was nearly the size of his head.

"Don't get it on your ears," Eleanor hissed at him, regretting that she had said she didn't want an ice cream. It looked delicious, but she knew she couldn't have one now. Someone might suspect she was having a good time.

Abraham was too busy licking even to notice what Eleanor said, but their mum had heard. "Eleanor," she warned.

Eleanor put on her headphones and turned up her CD player. She sighed for what seemed to be the millionth time that morning. It was going to be a very long day.

CHAPTER 2

GOLDTOWN FEVER

The car park outside Goldtown was almost full when they arrived, even though it was still early in the day. Usually busy car parks made her father irritable and he would mutter to himself. Today, Eleanor noticed, he was whistling away happily.

Abraham had finished his ice cream and was jiggling with anticipation again. Even Mum looked happy. Eleanor scowled.

"Did you know that the largest gold nugget ever found in the United

States weighed more than 22 kilograms?" asked Eleanor's dad as he finally found an empty space and pulled into it. Eleanor knew that he wasn't really asking though. He realized he was the only one in the car who knew stuff like that.

"Oh boy," muttered Eleanor, her head slumped against the car window. All she could think about was that Sally was going to see the hottest new comedy with her family in the afternoon. All the kids in her class had seen it, but Eleanor hadn't.

"How big is that, Dad?" asked Abraham. Eleanor leapt out of the car so that she wouldn't have to hear the answer.

★ ★ ★

The family lined up, got their tickets, and walked through the turnstile. Abraham sprang into action and immediately began dragging Dad by the hand.

"Wow, look at the funny buildings," he yelled. Eleanor noticed that the people around them were smiling. "He's not cute.

Look at those ears," she wanted to yell. But her mum was standing next to her, so she didn't.

"Doesn't it look amazing, Eleanor?" asked Dad.

Eleanor looked around. One wide, dusty street ran down the middle of the town. Both sides of the street were lined with

old brick buildings. At the far end, Eleanor could see what looked like a small schoolhouse with a steep roof and a bell. In front of it were see-saws and the only trees in the entire town. She wondered what the schoolhouse looked like inside. Goldtown did look pretty interesting, although Eleanor wasn't about to say so. She didn't want to give Dad the satisfaction.

Mum, Dad, and Abraham headed for the sheriff's office. "Come and see this wanted poster, Eleanor!" demanded Abraham.

"Billy Humbug: Train Robber," read Eleanor. "Billy Humbug," she said, snorting. "What kind of name is that?"

"He was a famous train robber," said Abraham. "They never caught him. And look, there are his lucky boots. He wore those when he robbed trains." Abraham sounded as if he were going to burst.

Eleanor looked where her brother was pointing. Sure enough, there was a pair of grimy brown leather cowboy boots in the display case.

Under the boots was a picture of a man. He had curly hair, like Abraham's. His eyes were mean slits, staring out from under the thickest, darkest, bushiest eyebrows Eleanor had ever seen.

"Look at his eyebrows," hooted Eleanor. "They look just like fluffy feather dusters."

Abraham giggled and Eleanor felt pleased, in spite of her bad mood.

"It's a shame they never caught him," said Dad, who had probably read the whole display twice, just in case he missed anything. "Back then, prospectors had a lot of trouble protecting their gold from thieves. They were vulnerable in many ways. Exposed to the elements, they lived a hard, solitary existence. There were also, of course, diseases..."

"Daaad!" protested Eleanor. She knew that somebody had to stop him, or they'd be standing there until the next giant gold nugget was discovered.

"Let's go and look at something else," demanded Eleanor. Without waiting for a reply, she marched off down the street and into the first building she came to.

CHAPTER 3

IN THE SPOTLIGHT

After the bright day outside, Eleanor blinked as she entered the darkened building. She wasn't sure where she was, but she could see a stage show going on. Someone shoved past her and made a beeline for the seats. It was Abraham, followed closely by Mum and Dad.

"Come on, Eleanor," hissed Abraham in a loud whisper. Knowing that Abraham was bound to insist loudly until she followed his lead, Eleanor sat down.

On the stage, a magician was pulling colourful scarves from his sleeve, and there was strange background music. It sounded weird, like a piano being played inside a tin can.

Abraham was twisting around in his seat beside Eleanor, trying to get a better view. Before either of them got a proper look, the music stopped and another man walked onto the stage. He wore a white shirt with a black ribbon tied at the neck.

"Put your hands together, folks, for the amazing Goldtown magician," cried the man enthusiastically into his microphone. The audience clapped politely, all except for Abraham, who clapped wildly.

"Now, have we got a volunteer to help with our next item?" asked the man.

Abraham's hand shot up into the air. "Over here," he shrieked.

Eleanor slid down in her seat just as a bright light swooped in from nowhere and settled on Abraham.

The man laughed. "Sorry, son," he said. "I should have said that we need a female volunteer." The audience chuckled with him. Abraham would be signing autographs next, thought Eleanor resentfully.

"Well, what about my sister, Eleanor?" asked Abraham.

People began turning in their seats to get a better view. Eleanor knew in an instant that she couldn't escape. There was nowhere she could hide.

"I'm going to kill you later," she hissed into Abraham's oversized left ear. Abraham smiled in reply, as if he had done her a favour. Sometimes Abraham's behaviour was hard for Eleanor to believe. "Just you wait," she added lamely. Eleanor was ready to say more, but the man on the stage interrupted her.

"Come on up, Elllleanooor!" cried the man. The audience began clapping.

With her face burning, Eleanor pushed awkwardly past the people in her row, and made her way slowly up to the stage. She felt sick, just as she did when she was about to sit a test.

"And how old are you, Eleanor?" asked the man, shoving his microphone right into her face.

Panic-stricken, Eleanor stared at his black ribbon. She had always hated being the centre of attention like this. All those people watching her – it was horrible.

Eleanor couldn't think. Her mind was spinning around like a bicycle wheel and her mouth was dry. She felt terribly hot. The only thing she could think about was that cool ice cream she had turned down earlier. She needed the space to think of something to say, but she couldn't get the ice cream out of her head.

Then something squeaked and the audience laughed. To her horror, Eleanor realized that she was the culprit! Her face burned even hotter. She couldn't begin to imagine how red she must be. She was certain she looked like a tomato. This was the worst thing that had ever happened to her. Ever!

Eleanor looked out into the glare of lights. She blinked, and tried to focus on something. She had to clear her head so that she could think!

In the strange mixture of harsh light and darkness, Eleanor could barely make out the front row of the audience. She searched for her family, but couldn't see them in the dark smudge of unknown faces. Eleanor realized that people weren't laughing any more. They were staring at her.

Eleanor had to get out of there! She pushed the microphone out of her face and ran blindly through the darkened theatre.

She kept running until she felt sunshine and fresh air.

CHAPTER 4

INTO THE WILD WEST

Eleanor stood very still, breathing deeply and trying to clear her head. When she finally felt well enough to look around, she immediately realized that things were about to get a whole lot worse.

There were people all around her – people talking and shopping and crossing the road and doing normal, everyday things. But these people didn't look like normal, everyday people. They were wearing clothes that Eleanor had seen only in the western movies that

Dad watched. They looked as if they had walked out of another century.

The women were all wearing long, full-sleeved dresses, gloves, and stiff hats, and they looked unreal – like giant dolls. The men were wearing hats, too, as well as braces and tall boots. Some men had skinny black ribbons around their necks, like the one the man on the stage had been wearing. Everyone looked very stern and proper.

A girl about the same age as Eleanor was leaning against a nearby post, feeding an apple to a horse. Eleanor didn't know what looked the strangest: the sight of a horse on the side of the street, or the girl's bonnet and long, heavy dress. She looked as if she belonged in a museum display, rather than real life.

Eleanor suddenly laughed, feeling very foolish – and relieved. Of course, this was all some kind of display! Goldtown was paying these people to dress up and walk around. Now that she had calmed down, it was obvious. She expected there could even

23

be a shoot-out at any moment. She hoped that Dad didn't miss it.

Wait until she told Sally all about this, thought Eleanor. The girl even looked like Sally, except for the hat. It must be irritating, the way it flopped over her face.

"Hey, don't you get hot in all that stuff?" called out Eleanor, walking over to her.

The girl looked up, startled. She had large grey eyes and her hair hung in black corkscrew ringlets. When she saw Eleanor, she seemed to forget all about the horse. Her hand dropped to her side and her mouth fell wide open. She gaped in shock, unable to speak.

Finally, the girl dropped her gaze and scurried into a nearby building, her ringlets bobbing. She seemed frightened. Eleanor felt dazed and slumped down on a bench next to the horse. She had never frightened anybody like that before. Her new-found confidence began to dissolve as rapidly as it had come. She felt her heart begin to pound again.

The street clattered and rumbled as horses passed, pulling carts of all sizes and descriptions. Eleanor watched as the dust rose in a cloud and slowly settled again with each passing cart. Something about what she

saw – the bizarre normality of it all – made Eleanor finally realize that, in some strange way, this was real life. It wasn't a theme park or a museum. She wished it was, because she certainly couldn't explain how or why this had happened.

All Eleanor knew was that it *had* happened, and that it was all too weird to think about. She couldn't think clearly anyway – even if she'd wanted to. But she knew she had to try and work out what was going on, no matter how confused she felt. Anything could happen. She had to keep her wits about her!

Eleanor started moving cautiously down the raised wooden footpath that lined the street. She made herself concentrate on the soft clopping noise of her shoes on the path and tried to ignore all the people who were slowing down and staring at her in amazement. You think *I* look strange? thought Eleanor.

A group of men stood by a rail, talking. They fell silent as Eleanor passed by. One man stared in fascination at her jeans and shoes. Their eyes met. Frightened that he was going to say something, Eleanor turned sharply through a doorway and under a sign worded:

It was a beautiful shop. On the shelves all about her were different-shaped bottles containing liquids of various colours. Other shelves displayed rolls of material, jars of buttons, and tin cups and plates.

In front of a wooden counter that ran the length of the shop stood barrels holding what looked like flour and sugar and many other dry goods that Eleanor couldn't quite identify. On the wall behind the counter hung tools for mining and gold panning.

The most beautiful things in the shop were the huge jars that stood at one end of the counter. They held what were obviously sweets: green sweets, red sweets, striped black-and-white sweets, all kinds of sweets. One particularly enormous jar held golden brown sweets shaped like tiny pillows.

Eleanor thought of Abraham and of how much he would have liked the sight of all those jars lined up in front of him. He would take a long time selecting sweets, thinking slowly and pointing carefully. For once, she didn't picture his enormous ears sticking out. She pictured his curls, which were rather like those of the man standing in front of one of the jars.

It seemed impossible, but Eleanor felt sure that she had seen the man somewhere before. There was something familiar about him, even though she couldn't see his face.

Eleanor slid quietly over by the counter to get a better look.

As soon as she saw his bushy eyebrows, Eleanor knew who it was. She wasn't fooled by his gold-rimmed glasses, which he hadn't worn in the photo. It was definitely Billy Humbug.

He paid for his sweets and turned to leave. And, as if to confirm her thoughts, Eleanor saw the sign in front of the jar where he had been standing. It read:

So Billy Humbug was real, and he had just been in the same shop as her!

Eleanor's head was spinning. This day was becoming more and more unbelievable! But she didn't care about that now. All she could think about was the famous train robber. She had to follow him!

Without another thought, Eleanor quietly slipped out of the shop, hot on the trail of Billy Humbug.

CHAPTER 5

HOT ON THE HUMBUG TRAIL

It seemed easier to be back out on the street this time. Perhaps it was because Eleanor expected to be stared at. Or perhaps it was the sense of purpose she felt as she worked to keep Humbug in her sight. She followed at a distance, careful to remain unnoticed. It wasn't very difficult. Humbug seemed very intent on his plans.

He headed down the street towards the small schoolhouse. Although he wasn't exactly hiding, he didn't seem to be going out of his way to be seen either. Humbug walked quickly, with his head down, keeping his hat tipped over his face. He kept well to the edge of the footpath as he passed a bank, a newspaper office, and a shop from which drifted the smell of leather.

It seemed to Eleanor that Humbug sped up momentarily as they passed what looked like the courthouse. Eleanor had to trot to keep him in sight. She felt almost like one of the horses on the street. It was hot work trying to keep up.

Humbug swung abruptly off the footpath at the corner by the schoolhouse. Eleanor reached the corner just in time to see him turn into a nearby building. Across its front were the faded words:

LIVERY STABLE

Unwilling to risk being caught in a small space with him again, Eleanor prowled around the building until she found a knothole in one of the wooden planks. Peering through, she saw Humbug with a horse – the most beautiful horse Eleanor had ever seen.

Humbug had left the stable door ajar, and a shaft of light was falling on the horse's coat. It shone a rich dark brown, so rich and dark that it looked almost black. Humbug was so enthralled with the horse that Eleanor felt she could have barged into the building and he wouldn't have noticed.

"How's my girl?" whispered Humbug, gently rubbing the horse's ears. He started to make soft snorting noises, as if he were a horse, too.

He was worse than Mum with her cat, thought Eleanor crossly. She certainly hadn't followed him just to hear this.

"It won't be long now, sweet Molasses," murmured Humbug.

It won't be long until what? Eleanor wondered to herself.

Humbug continued to study Molasses. Then he carefully inspected each hoof, and

finished with a look at the horse's teeth. Eleanor was amused. It wasn't as if Molasses ran on her teeth!

"That's my girl," said Humbug, and, with one last loving pat, he turned and left.

Up until Humbug's visit to the stables, Eleanor had followed him on a whim. She had no evidence against him. All she had was a notion that he was up to something.

Now she knew that he had a plan. What it was exactly, she couldn't say. But there was something purposeful in the way he was walking around the town that made Eleanor feel suspicious.

The words "Train Robber" ran across Eleanor's mind and she thought of the boots she had seen on display outside the sheriff's office. Was he wearing those boots today? It seemed impossible to imagine that Humbug was going to rob a train, but what else could he be planning to do? Eleanor had no idea what train robbers did in their spare time. It wasn't something they had covered in school. Whatever he was up to, Eleanor felt compelled to follow. She knew that, if she didn't hurry, she would lose him.

Peering cautiously around the corner of the stable, Eleanor could see Humbug striding up a side street. For the second time that day, she followed him.

The sun was now much higher in the sky, but Eleanor didn't want to take off her sweatshirt for fear of attracting even more attention – if that were possible. All of the women and girls had their arms covered with long sleeves. Eleanor didn't know how they could stand it. It was sweltering.

Had the sun been hotter back then? wondered Eleanor. Or rather "back now", she corrected herself. Eleanor couldn't help smiling at the craziness of it all.

And it wasn't just the heat that was bothering Eleanor. It was the dust, too! She could feel the dust in her eyes and in her ears. No doubt it was up her nose as well. She felt dirtier than she ever had before.

Suddenly, Humbug stopped walking and looked around. Eleanor ducked behind a tree. She waited for a moment, then peered around the trunk.

Humbug stood in the street, wiping his brow with a handkerchief. At first, Eleanor thought he had stopped because he was hot. But she soon saw that he, too, was watching and waiting.

From behind the tree, she poked out her head as far as she dared, so that she could keep an eye on him. Whatever he was doing, she hoped that he took his time, because the cool shade was bliss. Eleanor thought longingly of her Dad's iced tea.

Across the street from Humbug was a small wooden house surrounded by a picket fence. The tidy house looked strange, almost lonely, in the barren landscape.

A man sitting in a rocking chair on the veranda had obviously been waiting for Humbug. He didn't seem to be in a hurry, though. He wore a pink undershirt with braces holding up his trousers and he was swaying in his chair in a very relaxed fashion, rubbing his chin.

The two men stared at one another in silence. Eleanor was starting to get impatient. "This makes no sense at all," she muttered. Billy Humbug was proving to be a big rip-off.

Suddenly, the man on the porch stood up. Eleanor snapped to attention. Just then, she heard a train whistle blow in the distance. She swallowed hard and looked over at the two men. A single word passed between them. Eleanor's heart gave a leap as everything fell into place.

Humbug appeared satisfied. Pulling his hat back down over his face, he walked off. The other man turned around and walked back into the house.

Eleanor considered the word that had just been spoken. It was the biggest, most significant word she had ever heard.

"Noon," she whispered.

CHAPTER 6

TICKETS, PLEASE!

So, thought Eleanor, Humbug must be going to rob the noon train. But, although she felt confident that she was right about Humbug's plans, she didn't have a clue what she should do about it.

Eleanor's brain was churning like a washing machine. How was a kid supposed to stop a train robber? For a start, she wasn't even in the right century! Tears filled her eyes. This was just too much. And it wasn't as if it was her problem.

Eleanor's mind flicked back to Molasses. Maybe she could just go back to the stable, get on the horse, and ride off into the sunset, like they did in the westerns she'd watched with her dad.

For the first time, Eleanor wished that her dad was here to tell her what to do. But then, somehow, she felt that she already knew the answer, after all.

Eleanor thought back to the things that her dad had said about the prospectors. The hard work, the loneliness, and the danger he had spoken of had all seemed so distant, as if they had never really happened at all. But now, Eleanor wasn't so sure. Being here changed things. Eleanor knew she wasn't exactly part of this life, but she had seen and heard things. She had responsibilities. She had to help. She had no choice.

Still not feeling very brave, Eleanor took off down the street in the direction from which the train whistle had sounded.

The railway station was easy to spot. It was a squat, red building with flowers planted along the front, the first flowers that Eleanor had seen since arriving.

The train had pulled in and was huffing steam into the sky. It was amazingly noisy.

The platform was crowded with people, all of them busy with packages and trunks. Eleanor had no difficulty slipping onto the train, but she worried about what she would do when the conductor came around asking for tickets.

She chose a window seat near the back of the train and nervously waited for the other passengers to find a seat. Most people avoided her, sitting as far away as they could. Eleanor guessed it was because she looked different to them. She wondered why wearing different clothes mattered so much. But maybe, thought Eleanor, there was something else she didn't understand.

The last woman to board the train looked horrified when she realized there was nowhere else to sit other than beside

Eleanor. Carrying a large bag, she puffed up the aisle, looking very flustered. Then she settled herself into the seat, trying to keep as far away from Eleanor as possible. It was extremely difficult, given the tight squeeze, but Eleanor was grateful. At least now she was partly shielded from the penetrating gaze of the other passengers.

With a great hiss, the train pulled out of the station. Everyone settled back into their seats for the journey, except for two men Eleanor could see standing at the front of the carriage. They looked important, and stood with their arms crossed and their boots firmly planted on the floor. When the train gave a lurch, which was often, the men would narrow their eyes in concentration as they tried to keep their balance.

There was definitely something about the two men that was different from the other passengers. Eleanor realized that they must be guarding the gold that Humbug intended to plunder – gold that only she knew was about to be stolen.

She sat up straight in her seat and forced herself to concentrate. What was she going to do?

"Tickets, please!"

Eleanor was jolted from her thoughts by the train conductor, who was making his way noisily down the aisle. She slumped down in her seat. She just knew there was going to be a scene.

CHAPTER 7

HIGH NOON

The conductor turned a cold, suspicious eye on Eleanor. "Ticket, please, Miss," he said, in a very efficient voice.

"I haven't got one," stammered Eleanor. Well, that was a brilliant reply, she thought. That's really going to save the day!

"I'm sorry," said the conductor, not looking very sorry at all. "No ticket means no ride."

Except for the regular click-clack of the moving train, there was no other sound. Eleanor could feel the other passengers staring at her, and she had to force herself to speak in the unnerving silence.

"There is something I've got to tell you," said Eleanor. "Something really bad is going to happen. This train is going to be robbed, and you've got to stop it."

The conductor stared at Eleanor in rising disbelief. "I don't know who you are, young lady, but you've got no ticket and you're off this train at the next station." He turned away as if his business was done.

"Kids!" he said to the lady next to Eleanor.

Eleanor was outraged. How dare he dismiss her as a mere kid when she was trying to help! Especially when none of this was her problem. Eleanor's anger helped her to find her voice. "You've got to listen to me," she insisted loudly.

People had stopped pretending to look out the window and were openly listening. If only the conductor would listen, too.

"Billy Humbug is going to rob this train," said Eleanor. "You've got to do something quickly."

The name Billy Humbug had an astounding effect. The air was suddenly electric. The lady sitting next to her gasped and the conductor grew pale. The two guards at the front stepped forward, their eyes now glued to Eleanor.

"B-b-billy H-h-humbug!" stammered the conductor.

"How do you know?" demanded the shorter of the two guards.

Eleanor knew that she had no time for long explanations. "I saw him in town. I followed him and overheard his plan. If you don't believe me, look for yourselves."

The tall guard immediately rushed to the back of the train. The people sat, transfixed, and the air was filled with expectation. Eleanor hoped that she was right. What would happen to her if she was wrong? She thought of the jail she had seen in the sheriff's office. They obviously used it.

Fortunately, the guard returned, putting an end to Eleanor's gloomy thoughts. He rushed up the aisle, his face flushed.

"Someone's coming," he shouted.

The train sprang to life. People began making preparations. Packages were pulled closer, children's coats were buttoned, and one old man even wound his pocket watch. Eleanor looked at her own watch. In three minutes' time, it would be high noon. She had played her part.

"Quick! Someone get a rope," ordered the tall guard. This didn't seem a particularly useful item to Eleanor, who was watching with fascination. People were scrambling around in a panic. "Rope! I need rope!" the guard reminded them, rather unnecessarily, thought Eleanor. Yelling wasn't going to find some any faster.

Amid all the chaos, the old man with the pocket watch sat quietly hunched over something, busy with a task. Looking closely, Eleanor saw that he was trying to untie a rope that was bound around his trunk. In all the rush and commotion, nobody had noticed him. His fingers were slow and clumsy.

Eleanor leaped from her seat and forced her way past the woman with the bag. "Over here!" she called to the tall guard.

The guard came over, pushing his way eagerly through the passengers. "Move aside. Move aside," he called – quite politely under the circumstances. In a few moments, he was by Eleanor's side, helping her to untie the rope.

"This will do," he said as they unwound the rope from around the trunk. But Eleanor still couldn't see why the guard was so anxious to get his hands on some rope.

The guard began to push his way back up the aisle, clutching the rope. The shorter guard hauled open the door, and they both stood there, framed by the rushing scenery.

The timing was perfect. Just as Humbug came galloping up alongside the train, it slowed almost to a stop, allowing the tall guard to throw a perfect loop of rope around Humbug's shoulders. He was jerked to the ground in a cloud of dust.

His beautiful horse didn't seem to notice that its load was lighter, and continued on without him. For a split second, Eleanor almost felt sorry for Humbug. He wouldn't be riding Molasses again for a long time.

The train screeched to a halt and the guards leaped to the ground and jumped on Humbug. The conductor appeared by their side, and tore off the handkerchief that Humbug had covered his face with. The robber looked furious, like a wild animal caught in a trap.

Any concern Eleanor might have felt for Billy Humbug was quickly replaced with concern for herself. The other passengers, very excited by Humbug's capture, were heading her way.

It was like being a movie star. Eleanor was surrounded. Everybody was trying to touch her. The air was filled with jabbering voices and seemed to be getting thinner and thinner. Eleanor was having a hard time breathing, and it was *so* hot.

The last thing that Eleanor remembered was the conductor's face pressed close to her own. "Are you all right, Miss?" he asked.

Eleanor tried to answer, but darkness swirled over her before she could.

CHAPTER 8

BACK IN THE SADDLE

The first thing Eleanor saw when she opened her eyes was Abraham's ears, with his small anxious face peering down between them.

"Are you all right, Eleanor? Wake up!" If Eleanor hadn't known better, she would have said that Abraham sounded worried.

Mum was definitely worried. "Eleanor!" she said, echoing Abraham.

Eleanor sat up.

"Slowly now. You had us worried there for a moment," said Dad.

"Daaad," groaned Eleanor. "You could be a bit more original."

"Well, you're obviously OK," said Mum, chuckling to Dad.

Am I OK? Eleanor asked herself. It felt good to be able to breathe properly. It felt good to be stared at for sitting on the footpath, and not for wearing weird clothes. And it felt good to be surrounded by her family. But there was a funny gap, sort of like how it felt when she lost her first tooth. A hole was there that felt as if it shouldn't be.

"Come on, Eleanor," said Mum. "I think we should get you home."

Eleanor looked around as they walked to the exit. The street was full of tourists with cameras around their necks, and kids in pushchairs. There were no horses, no women in bonnets and long, heavy dresses, and no Billy Humbug. Had there ever been?

As they passed the sheriff's office, Eleanor saw the display they had seen when they first arrived. It stood there as if nothing had happened. But, looking more closely, Eleanor

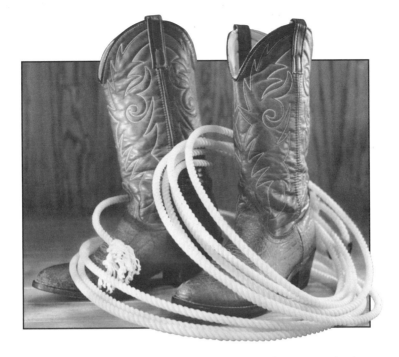

saw that it *was* different. Coiled around the cowboy boots was a rope, and next to the picture of Billy Humbug was a picture of the tall guard from the train, smiling proudly.

Eleanor didn't have to read the words to know what they said. Humbug had been stopped and the gold had not been stolen.

Looking at the guard smiling down at her from the display, Eleanor decided that it hadn't been such a bad trip after all!

FROM THE AUTHOR

I live in Wellington, New Zealand, a small island country. Maybe that's why I'm so interested in travel.

I have always thought the idea of time travel is wonderful, which is one of the reasons I wrote this story.

I know if I had a choice of where to go, I wouldn't be able to decide. I hope that, if I ever do get to go somewhere, it will happen to me the same way it happened to Eleanor!

Susan Paris

FROM THE PHOTOGRAPHER

Ever since I was thirteen years old I've wanted to be a photographer. Today I take photographs for books, magazines, catalogues, and many other projects. My career has taken me to a lot of places around the United States, from Phoenix to Chicago, Dallas, Atlanta, and Denver. Photographing this story was like going back home to the "Old West" in Arizona.

Mary Foley

DISCUSSION STARTERS

1. Eleanor seems resentful of her father for making her go on this trip, and of her brother just for being there. What do you think about her attitude? How well do you think her parents handled her moods?

2. The story ends with Eleanor seeing the altered poster. How else could the author have chosen to end this story?

3. Eleanor feels totally out of place in the past, especially with what she is wearing. This can also happen in real time. Can you think of a time when you felt "out of place"? How did you respond to it?